5/21/98

Dear Alex,

Thank you for your patience – Hope you enjoy "Just Too Little"

Sincerely,

Georgia McGuire

# JUST TOO LITTLE

BY GINA AND MERCER MAYER

A GOLDEN BOOK • NEW YORK
Western Publishing Company, Inc., Racine, Wisconsin 53404


Library of Congress Catalog Card Number: 92-74675 ISBN: 0-307-23191-7 A MCMXCIII

My little sister wants to do everything I do, but sometimes she's just too little.

I was playing with my racetrack.
My little sister said, "Can I play, too?"
I said, "No, you're too little."

She wanted to play with my marbles,
but I said, “You’re too little for marbles.”

So she asked to play with my
Super Critter video game instead.
I said, “You’re too little for that, too.”

Mom said, “She’s not too little for everything.”
So I let my sister play with my truck.
The wheel was broken anyway.

When my friends came over, they wanted to play cops and robbers. My little sister wanted to play, too. I said, "You're too little."

We hid until my
sister went inside.

We had a race.
My sister said, "Can I race, too?"
I said, "You're too little."
She said, "Please?"
So we let her say, "On your mark.
Get set. Go!"

We made a spaceship out of a big
paper box and played astronaut critters.
My sister said, “Can I play?”
I said, “You’re too little to go to the moon.”

But we let her help us land.

When we were skateboarding,
my little sister said, “Can I skate, too?”
I let her try.

She fell down and hurt her knee.
I knew she was just too little.
Mom had to fix up her knee.

We climbed high up in a tree.
My sister said, "Can I come up?"
I said, "You're too little to
come up this far."

So I helped her climb up
on a low branch.

We wanted to walk to the store to get a snack. I knew my little sister was too little to go. We had to sneak away.

But I brought her back some bubble gum. She got it in her fur.
I guess she's just too little for gum.

Then we tried to catch tadpoles in the ditch.
My sister said, "Can I catch some, too?"
I thought she was too little, but I
let her anyway.

She fell in the ditch and got all muddy.
We took her in the house to get cleaned up.
I knew she was too little.

I played tag with my friends.
My sister said, "Can I play tag?"
I said, "You're too little."
We let her sit at home base and watch.

Then we decided to play baseball
with some other critters in the park.
But we needed one more person to
play. My sister said, "Can I play?"

I said, “But you’re too little.”
Mom said, “Let her play.”
I made her play on the other team.

She hit a home run!

My sister is too little to do most
of the things that I like to do.
But she's not too little to play
on my team . . . next time.